Pittman, Samuel E., II,
Alligator jazz /
[2018]
33305244509687
mi   03/14/19

ALLIGATOR JAZZ

SAMUEL E. PITTMAN II

ILLUSTRATED BY SHEILA BAILEY

PELICAN PUBLISHING COMPANY

GRETNA 2018

Copyright © 2018
By Samuel E. Pittman II

Illustrations copyright © 2018
By Sheila Bailey
All rights reserved

The word "Pelican" and the depiction of a pelican are
trademarks of Pelican Publishing Company, Inc., and are
registered in the U.S. Patent and Trademark Office.

Library of Congress Cataloging-in-Publication Data

Names: Pittman, Samuel E., II, author. | Bailey, Sheila, illustrator.
Title: Alligator jazz / by Samuel E. Pittman II ; illustrated by Sheila
    Bailey.
Description: Gretna : Pelican Publishing Company, 2018. | Summary: Alligator
    Slim gives up the blues, moves to the city, and gets a job playing jazz
    saxophone at the zoo, but fellow performer Weasel is not happy about his
    success.
Identifiers: LCCN 2018004582| ISBN 9781455624225 (hardcover : alk. paper) |
    ISBN 9781455624232 (ebook)
Subjects: | CYAC: Musicians--Fiction. | Jazz--Fiction. | Alligators--Fiction.
    | Weasels--Fiction. | Zoos--Fiction.
Classification: LCC PZ8.3.P558684155 All 2018 | DDC [E]--dc23 LC record available
at https://lccn.loc.gov/2018004582

Printed in Malaysia

Published by Pelican Publishing Company, Inc.
1000 Burmaster Street, Gretna, Louisiana 70053
www.pelicanpub.com

All praise, glory, and honor to the living God and to His Son, Jesus Christ, my Lord and Savior!

To Samuel (Sr.) and Floydie Pittman, my father and mother, for your love and encouragement—I am blessed to be your son!

To O. C. and Nellie Pittman (Paw-Paw and Grandmamma) and to Floyd and Clara Woodfork (Daddy Floyd and Mama Clara), for your faithfulness.

To Mrs. Mackie Meyer, my third-grade teacher at Somerville Elementary, for letting me read when I was finished with my work. To everyone who has encouraged me along this journey.

To every kid with a notebook and a pen and a heart full of ideas—write!—S. P. II

For Mom, who loved music!—S. B.

All the swamp critters were shocked by the news—
Alligator Slim gave up the blues!
"I've sung about bad times, sad times, and pain.
I've sung about droughts and hurricanes.

I've sung the blues slow, and I've sung the blues fast,
but I'm laying down the blues—I'm picking up jazz!

I have no more down-and-out, so-sad ditties."
Alligator Slim grabbed his sax and his hat
and headed for the city.

Alligator found a spiffy place to stay.
"I'll get me some shut-eye, and tomorrow I'll play."
When the sun came up, Alligator went to The Zoo.

He auditioned for the manager, who said, "Alligator Slim, the audience will definitely dig you!"

"My first city gig! This place is all right!"
Alligator bought a new suit, a new hat, and cleaned up for that night.

The announcer greeted, "Good evening! Hello!
Thank you for coming to enjoy our show!
You'll hear your favorites: 'Sticks, Weasel, and Rhino Jim—
But first, let me introduce to you . . . Alligator Slim!"

"Evenin', folks! Sit back and relax!"
Then Alligator Slim went to town on his sax.
They listened. They smiled. They took in the sound—
Alligator Slim was gettin' down!

But Weasel turned green—"He's stealing my fans!
I'll fix that 'Gator—I have just the plan!"

After the show, the musicians got together to relax, and while Alligator was distracted . . . away went his sax!

"My sax! It's gone!" Alligator declared.
They looked all around, but the sax wasn't there.

Alligator Slim was sad, sad, sad.
He groaned, "This is bad, bad, bad!"

Alligator Slim was in a terrible bind!
The days went by, but his sax he did not find.

His hopes were low, and his money was too,
so Alligator Slim decided what he would do.

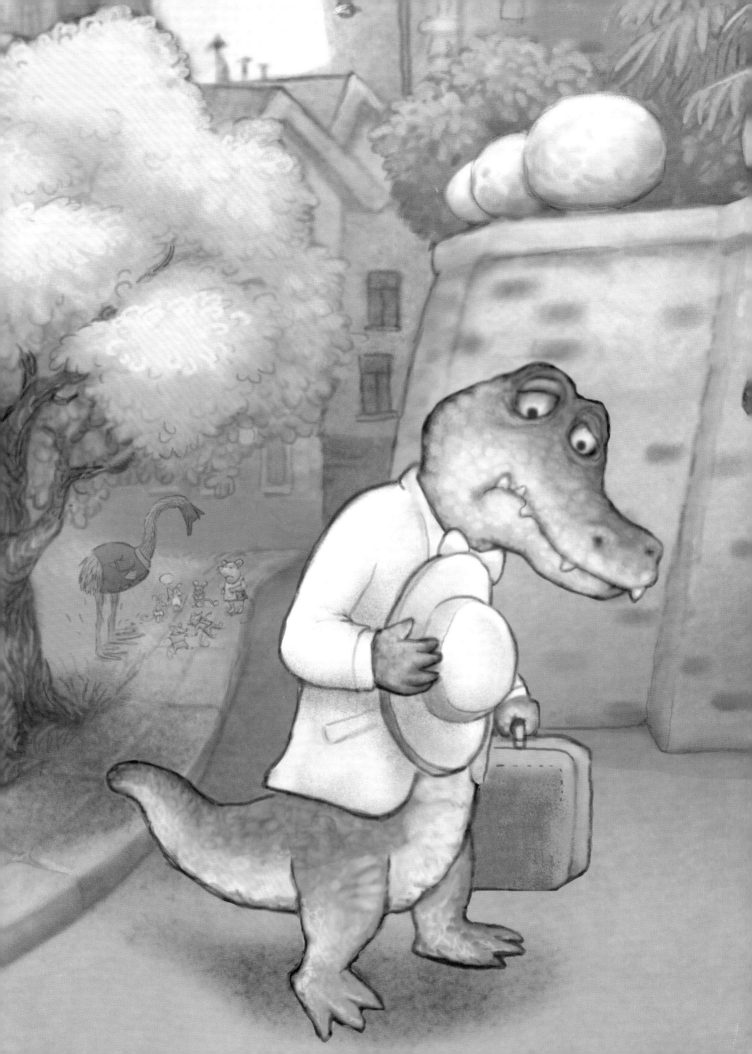

He sighed to himself, "I have no sax to play.
I'll go back to the blues, in the swamp I will stay."
But Alligator wanted to hear that jazz just once more.
He went to The Zoo and stood by the door.

Weasel went up to play—
with Alligator's sax!

"Listen, folks!" Weasel said.
"Sit back and relax!"

He screeched and he blared and
the audience moaned.

"He's hurting our ears with that bad
saxophone!"

"That sax is all right!" said Alligator Slim.
He walked up to Weasel and snatched the sax from him.

Alligator Slim played that sax like a dream—the crowd was satisfied and the sound was serene.

They clapped and they cheered—and Weasel did too!

"I'm sorry," he apologized. Alligator replied, "I forgive you."

"Now the city's my home, and my music is jazz!"
And he stayed and he played on that sax with pizzazz!

When all the swamp critters heard the news,
they went to the city, by foot and by cruise,
by wheels and by wings they came to the show
and watched Alligator Slim pick up that sax

AND BLOW!

AUTHOR'S NOTE

Jazz is a musical art form that can be played on a variety of instruments, including the saxophone, and it can be played in a variety of ways, from slow to fast, from a composed song (already written) to improvisation (the musicians make up parts of a song as they play). Jazz musicians can play in big bands and they can play in small groups, such as trios or quartets, and many jazz songs feature a solo by one of the musicians. Jazz isn't limited to instruments only—jazz vocalists (singers) sing lyrics as the musicians play, and the combination is indeed snazzy!

Perhaps Alligator Slim will form a jazz group with other musicians who play at The Zoo, and perhaps they'll even add a vocalist, too!